ICARUS
THE BOY WHO
FLEW TOO
HIGH

Retold by Katie Daynes

Illustrated by Kim Smith

Reading consultant: Alison Kelly

Contents

Chapter 1

Prisoners

"I'm so bored," moaned Icarus. "Bored, bored, boring old bored."

His dad, Daedalus, said nothing. He was busy at his desk, scribbling.

I think I'm onto something...

Icarus took a sheet of parchment, folded it and threw it across the room.

"Hey!" cried his dad, finally looking up. "Why did you do that?"

"There's nothing else *to* do," said Icarus. "We've been cooped up here for months."

"Well," said Daedalus proudly. "I might just have a plan to get us out."

Icarus sighed. "It was your brilliant plan that got us here in the first place..."

Daedalus had designed the world's most complicated maze for King Minos of Crete.

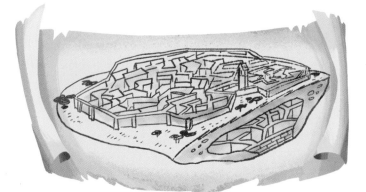

Then, three months ago, he helped one of the king's prisoners to escape from the maze.

King Minos was furious. He locked Daedalus and Icarus in the maze's tall tower.

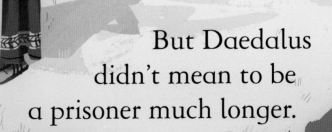

And you're never coming out!

But Daedalus didn't mean to be a prisoner much longer.

Chapter 2

The escape plan

Attach a rope
to an arrow.

Use a bow
to fire it.

"Ha! What bow?" said
Icarus, looking around the
room. "What arrow? What
rope? We might as well make
some wings and fly away!"

12

Daedalus raced back to his
desk and began to scribble
again excitedly.

"Ta dah!" he said at last.
Icarus looked at the latest
plan and frowned.

"That looks like you and
me..." he said, "with wings."
"Exactly!"

"And where do we get *them* from?" asked Icarus.

"We make them of course," replied Daedalus.

"All we need
are vines from
the wall for
the frames...

...feathers
to make
the wings...

...and wax from
our candles
to stick them
together."

16

"The birds won't just *give* us their feathers," Icarus said.

Daedalus thought hard. "We could tempt them to the windowsill with bread, and collect any feathers that fall?"

17

It wasn't a great plan, but it was the best one they had.

The next day, when the guard brought breakfast, they set aside half of their bread.

Chapter 3

Feeding the birds

"Fresh breadcrumbs!" called
Daedalus. "Come and get
them, birdies."

By the end of the first day, Daedalus had collected three feathers – and Icarus's tummy was rumbling.

Well, it's a start.

What a waste of bread!

By the end of the second day, Daedalus had collected nine more feathers...

...and Icarus's tummy was grumbling.

After a week, they had collected seventy feathers.

After two weeks, they had over two hundred.

Let's hope the guards don't spot them.

A month later, they had enough feathers to start making the wings.

Icarus had the dangerous task of pulling vines from the tower.

One more piece should do it.

As he tore off the last piece,
he sent a stone tumbling down
to the guards below.

Daedalus shaped the vines into two sturdy frames.

One by one, he stuck the feathers on with melted wax.

"Tomorrow we can have a test flight," said Daedalus.

"I was afraid you might say that," said Icarus.

Chapter 4

The test flight

"Wake up!" called Daedalus, shaking his son by the shoulder.

"But it's not even morning," moaned Icarus.

"We don't want the guards to know," said Daedalus. "Now put your arms through here, and here."

Nobody can see you.

I look silly.

"What do I do now?" said
Icarus. "Just wave my arms
and jump up and down?"

"I think we might need to
jump off something," said
Daedalus. "Here, help me
to pile up the furniture."

So, in a corner of their prison room, Daedalus and Icarus built a practice tower.

"You first!" said Icarus.

Daedalus climbed carefully
to the top of the tower.

He wobbled,

fell,

flapped

and flew!

"I want to try!" cried Icarus,
clambering up the furniture.

Soon he was soaring around too, bumping into walls and dive-bombing his dad.

This is fun!

"What's all the noise?" came a guard's gruff voice from below.

Daedalus and Icarus crashed to the ground.

"Just, erm, spring cleaning," said Daedalus, spitting out a feather.

The guard left their breakfast and stomped down the stairs.

Sorry! None for you today.

"Whew, that was close," said Daedalus, checking the wings for damage.

"That was great!" cried Icarus, with a big grin.

Daedalus hugged his son. "Tomorrow morning we'll fly away from this prison forever."

Chapter 5

Flying free

This time, Icarus didn't mind waking up early. He silently slipped on his wings and joined his dad at the window.

"It's a long way down,"
Icarus whispered.

"But we're not going down," said his dad, smiling. "These wings will take us over the sea to freedom!"

"You first," said Icarus.

"Remember to hold your arms out wide," said Daedalus, "and don't fly too near the sun. We don't want to melt the wax."

OK Dad.

Icarus watched his dad launch himself from the window ledge. At first he seemed to be falling...

...but soon the wind caught his wings and he was soaring.

"Wait for me!" cried Icarus.
He took a deep breath, and
leaped from the window,
flapping hard to catch up.

I can fly!

Far behind, two guards stood
shaking their fists, but there
was nothing they could do.

"The sheep are so tiny!" cried
Icarus, zooming higher. "And
the tower is just a twig!"
He swooped after his dad
and out over the sparkling sea.

"Stay close," called Daedalus. "And keep away from the sun."

But Icarus was too excited to listen. He skimmed over the waves, feeling cool spray on his face.

Then he swerved up into the sky, feeling the hot sun on his back, the wind in his hair, the joy of so much space.

Higher and higher and higher he went, until he was just a blur in the blue.

A feather floated down past Daedalus. "Icarus?" he called.
Then another.
"Icarus!" he shouted.
Then several more.

In a panic, Daedalus
searched the sky for his son.

ICARUS!

Next he searched the sea.
He flew high and low, calling
for Icarus, until his arms ached
and his voice was hoarse.

All he found were a few
feathers scattered on the water.

"Oh Icarus," he whispered.
"You flew too high! But now
you are free forever."

About the story

The story of Daedalus and Icarus was first told around 3,000 years ago in Ancient Greece. The sea by the island of Crete is named after Icarus. It's called the Icarian Sea.

Designed by Sam Whibley
Series editor: Lesley Sims
Series designer: Russell Punter

First published in 2016 by Usborne Publishing Ltd., Usborne House, 83-85 Saffron Hill, London EC1N 8RT, England. www.usborne.com
Copyright © 2016 Usborne Publishing Ltd.